The Little Match Girl

For a free color catalog describing Gareth Stevens' list of high-quality
children's books, call 1-800-341-3569 (USA) or 1-800-461-9120 (Canada).

Quality Time™ Classics

Tales of Hans Christian Andersen

The Little Match Girl
The Steadfast Tin Soldier
The Top and the Ball
The Woman with the Eggs

Library of Congress Cataloging-in-Publication Data

Erickson, Jon, 1951-
    The little match girl.

    (Quality time classics)
    Adaptation of: Den lille pige med svovlstikkerne.
    Summary: The wares of the poor little match girl illuminate her cold world, bringing some beauty to her
brief, tragic life.
    [1. Fairy tales] I. Andersen, H. C. (Hans Christian), 1805-1875. Lille pige med svovlstikkerne. II.
Mogensen, Jan, ill. III. Title. IV. Series.
PZ8.E69Li   1987   [E]   87-42585
ISBN 1-55532-342-1
ISBN 1-55532-317-0 (lib. bdg.)

This North American edition first published in 1987 by

Gareth Stevens Children's Books
1555 North RiverCenter Drive, Suite 201
Milwaukee, Wisconsin 53212, USA

Printed in the United States of America

2 3 4 5 6 7 8 9 96 95 94 93 92 91 90

The Little Match Girl

by Hans Christian Andersen

retold by Jon Erickson
illustrations by Jan Mogensen

Gareth Stevens Children's Books
MILWAUKEE

It was snowing and the cold was cruel.
It was growing dark on the last evening of the
year, New Year's Eve.

Through the cold and dark streets walked a
poor little girl, with no hat and no shoes.

Her bare feet were red and blue with the cold.
In her apron she carried a bunch of matches
to sell, and she carried some in her hand, too.
No one had bought any matches from her all
day. No one had given her one thin dime.

She shivered as she crept along, the snowflakes
covering her long blonde hair.
Poor little girl!
The windows of the houses were all filled with
light and she smelled the delicious smell of
roast goose.

"It's New Year's Eve," she thought.

In a corner where two houses met she sat
down and tucked her little feet under her.
Now the little match girl was even colder.
She did not dare to go home, for she had sold
no matches and her father would beat her for
it.

Anyway, it was cold at home. They lived in
the attic under the roof, and the wind blew
right through.
Oh! A match might do some good!
She could strike it on the wall and warm her
hands.

She took a match and struck it on the brick wall next to her. R-r-r-r-atch! How it sputtered and flashed! It burned just like a candle. She held her cold hands over the warm little light.

The little girl felt like she was sitting before a big warm stove with brass fixtures. It felt so safe and comforting.

Then the match went out.

And the stove was gone. There she sat with the burnt end of a match in her hand.

She lit a second match.
The flame lit up the wall and the wall
disappeared. She could see right through into
a dining room. On the table was a snow-white
tablecloth. At all the places were shining
plates and glasses.
A stuffed goose jumped down from the table
and waddled across the floor, a knife and fork
in its back. It shuffled right up to the little
match girl.

Her flame went out and all she saw was the
cold gray wall in front of her.

She struck a third match.
The flame became a giant Christmas tree.
She sat beneath a tree more beautifully
trimmed than those she had seen in the
windows of stores. A thousand candles burned
in its green branches. Ornaments glowed and
gazed down at her.
She reached her hand toward them —

— and the match went out. The Christmas tree faded away and its candles turned to stars in the sky. One of them fell, with a long trail of fire.

"Someone is dying," said the little girl.

Her grandmother, who had died, who had loved her, had told her that when a star fell to the earth, someone's soul rose up to heaven.

She scratched another match against the wall.
In the brightness of its light she saw her
Grandma, shining clear, sweet, and kindly.

"Grandma!" shouted the little girl. "Oh, take
me with you! I know you will leave when the
match burns out. Just like the stove, the roast
goose, and the beautiful Christmas tree."

The little girl lit all her matches at once, for she thought that she could keep her Grandma that way.

The matches all burned bright as day.

Grandma was so big and so beautiful. The little match girl felt herself lifted up in Grandma's arms, flying up to where there's no cold and there's no fear — up to heaven.

In the morning she was found, her cheeks red and her lips smiling.
She had frozen to death, against the wall in the corner, on the last night of the Old Year. Her lap was full of burnt-out matches.

"She tried to get warm," people said.

No one knew what beauty the little match girl had seen.

No one knew with what glory she rose with her Grandma into the New Year.

THE END